...introducing

Benji-Bat

Slobberchops

Bast

Unicorn

Lily

Windy

Welcome to Sleepy Land...

1

A girl and her dog lay curled up in bed.
Someone turned off the light
and then it was night.

The dog was puzzled. He looked under the pillow.
'Not there,' he said.
He looked under the bed. 'Not there,' he said.
He looked up at the ceiling - and shook his head.
'Lily - Where is Sleepy Land?' he asked.
'Is it in your bed?'

'Shhhh! It's a secret!' giggled Lily,
'Who told you that?'
'You did,' said Slobberchops.
'You said, "Lets go to Sleepy Land"
– and now we are in bed!'

'Sleepy Land is lovely,' sighed Lily,
'It's where dreams come alive. I dream I'm playing.'
'With who?'
'With you, Slobberchops. With you!'

'And can we play with Windy the Fairy?'
'Oh yes!'
'And the naughty bat, Benji-Bat?'
'Oh yes!'
'And Bast, the snooty cat?'
'Oh yes! When our magic friends come,
we'll all have lots and lots of fun!'
'So Sleepy Land is....

Fairy-tale Land! But will we play with a unicorn?'
'Oh yes! Puff! Puff! Puff! Windy sprinkles her magic dust.
Then Bast jumps onto the unicorn's back!'
'And Benji-Bat? Does he jump onto the unicorn too?'
'The magic bat's wings go flap, flap, flap.'
'Then what does he do?'

'He swings round and round on the unicorn's tail!
Twit-twoo! Twit-twoo!'

'Sleepy Land is a magic place.
We play all day and all night too!
Then Benji-Bat says, "If I'm right - and I am because
I'm always right,
- it's time to sleep in Sleepy Land.
Twit-twoo! Twit-twoo!"'

'So, Sleepy Land is... Wonderland?
Wow! Oh Lily! Take me there. Now!'
'Close your eyes,' whispered Lily.'
She tickled his ears, and stroked his brow.
'And the magic will happen, right here, and right now!'
They both closed their eyes, until...

'Chilly-wum-dum. Chilly-wum-do!' In a burst of
magic dust, the unicorn, the cat and the fairy arrived!
'Meeeow! Good day to you,' said the cat.
And she took a bow. 'Have you come here to play?'
'Oh yes! Sleepy Land is Wonderland!' giggled Lily.
'We're going to sing and dance and play all day!'
Slobberchops' eyes opened wide. 'It's magic!' he said.
A unicorn, pretty and proud,
was dancing and prancing all over the bed!
'Meeeow! sang the cat as she jumped on its back,
'Yeeeha!' sang Benji-Bat as he swung on its tail.
'It's a magical day!'

'Are we dreaming Lily?'
asked Slobberchops. 'What have you done?'
Lily giggled. 'I don't know! But I think we are inside
a fairy tale. And we're just having fun!'
They played all day and all night too.
Then Benji-bat said, 'If I'm right
and I am because I'm always right,
it's time to sleep in Sleepy Land.
Twit-twoo! Twit-twoo!'

A girl and her dog lay curled up in bed.
Someone turned on the light
And...
then it was bright.

Colour me in

Colour me in